Naughty Little Puppy

A Home for Rascal

Woof!
Woof!
Woof!

For William ~ H.W.
For Mum and Lucy ~ K.P.

WOOF
magazine

STRIPES PUBLISHING
An imprint of Magi Publications
1 The Coda Centre,
189 Munster Road,
London SW6 6AW

A paperback original
First published in Great Britain
in 2010

Text copyright © Holly Webb, 2010
Illustrations copyright
© Kate Pankhurst, 2010
Cover photographs copyright
© Lifeonwhite.com, 2010

ISBN: 978-1-84715-128-5

The right of Holly Webb and Kate
Pankhurst to be identified as the
author and illustrator of this work
respectively has been asserted by
them in accordance with the
Copyright, Designs and Patents
Act, 1988.

A CIP catalogue record for this
book is available from the British
Library.

Printed and bound in the UK.

10 9 8 7 6 5 4 3 2 1

My Naughty Little Puppy

Holly Webb

Illustrated by
Kate Pankhurst

stripes

Chapter One

Wonderful News

"You mean it? A real puppy?" Ellie whispered, smiling so wide that it almost hurt. She had been asking for a dog for ages, ever since her sixth birthday, which was just a bit more than two years ago. Auntie Gemma had given her a book about dogs, with pictures of all the different breeds. From then on, Ellie had been desperate to have a dog. But Mum and Dad had always said things like *I don't think we've got the space* and *not*

My Naughty Little Puppy

till you're older. This was a total surprise.

There was so much noise in the kitchen after Dad's big announcement that he didn't actually hear what Ellie said, although he couldn't miss the smile.

"Now we just have to decide what sort of dog we want," said Dad.

My Naughty Little Puppy

Ellie's older brother Max was yelling
and jumping around. "We need a really
big dog! One we can run in the park with."
And her big sister Lila was tugging on
Dad's sleeve. "A red setter – they're
gorgeous, and they've got fur the same
colour as my hair!"

My Naughty Little Puppy

Ellie frowned. Just like Lila to want a dog
to make her look pretty, as if it was a new
bracelet or something! Anyway, Lila was
beautiful already. Lots of people who had
red hair didn't like it, and people teased
them – all the boys at Ellie's school called
her Ginger – but no one ever called Lila
names. They wouldn't dare.

"We'll talk about it when I get home
from work," said Dad. "I've got to go now,
or I'll be late. Bye, all of you! Don't drive
Mum mad!" It was only the end of the first
week of the Easter holidays, and Ellie's
mum had already joked that she couldn't
wait for them to go back to school.

Ellie looked down at the drawing she'd
been doing. Her dog magazine had a

gorgeous Jack Russell on the cover, and
she'd been trying to copy it.
It seemed a pity that Lila
and Max both wanted to
have a big dog. She had
been hoping for a more cuddly
sort of puppy. Something small,
that she could pick up. Maybe it would
even sleep on the end of her bed! A red
setter would hardly fit in Ellie's tiny room!

Lila started rooting through Ellie's pencil
case. "Please can you draw me a red
setter, Ellie? Here, if you mix the orange
and the brown crayon together, it'll be the
right colour."

"I can't remember what they look like,"
Ellie muttered.

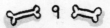

My Naughty Little Puppy

"You know you can draw anything. You're so clever!" Lila beamed at her. "Please! I can describe one. Um. Floppy fur and a long, feathery tail."

Ellie began to draw a dog that wasn't really any particular kind.

"No, the fur's a sort of orangier colour than that." Lila held out the end of her ponytail. "Almost the same colour as mine, look."

My Naughty Little Puppy

Max peered over at the drawing. "That's good, Ellie. But we don't want one of those fluffy dogs. Think of all the brushing!"

Lila sniffed. "Some of us don't mind brushing our hair. It's only you that doesn't know what a comb looks like."

Ellie ignored them as they started arguing. Lila and Max were only a year apart and they fought all the time, although it had got a bit better since Lila started secondary school. Ellie went on drawing, but she still didn't think she'd got the red setter quite right. She'd have to look it up in her dog book later. Still, Lila seemed to like it, and she went off to put the drawing on the pinboard in her bedroom.

My Naughty Little Puppy

Suddenly, there was a loud banging and scrabbling at the front door, and Ellie dashed along the hall, calling to her mum, who was hidden away in the little room under the stairs where she kept her computer.

"I think it's Christy, Mum, can I go for a walk with her and Bouncer?"

Bouncer was a big golden Labrador who belonged to Ellie's best friend Christy, and most mornings during the holidays Ellie went to the park with them. Mum poked her head round the door and smiled at her. "Course you can. Just think – it won't be long before you can take our dog with you, Ellie!"

Ellie grinned back. That would be absolutely perfect.

Chapter Two

The Perfect Dog

Ellie was almost dancing as she and Christy set off down the road. The park wasn't far from Ellie's house. Christy only lived round the corner too, so she was allowed to walk Bouncer there on her own, or with Ellie.

"What's up with you?" Christy asked.

"We're getting a dog!" Ellie told her, beaming.

"Really? That's brilliant!" Christy stopped dead, accidentally jerking Bouncer's lead

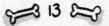

My Naughty Little Puppy

so he stopped, too. He looked up at her, confused.

"I know! I can't believe they finally said yes!"

"What sort are you going to get?" Christy asked. "A Lab like Bouncer?"

My Naughty Little Puppy

"We haven't decided. Dad said we'd talk about it tonight. Max wants a big dog, and Lila wants a red setter, but I like little dogs." She leaned over to pat Bouncer. "I love you, Bouncer! But I'd like a dog I can cuddle."

Ellie sighed. "When I dreamed about having a dog I didn't really think about having to share it with Max and Lila. Max is so sporty, he'll want to do all the walks, and Lila will do all the grooming. She'll be painting its claws pink! I won't get to do anything!"

Christy shook her head. "I'm not so sure. Max is really loud. Dogs don't like loud, Ellie, 'specially not when they're puppies. They like gentle, cuddly people. Like you. I bet most

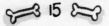

dogs would be scared of Lila, too. *I'm
scared of her!*" Bouncer tugged hopefully
on his lead and Christy started walking
again. "And Bouncer loves you. He doesn't
like everybody, you know."

"You think so? The puppy might really
like me?" Ellie asked hopefully.

Christy nodded. "I should think your
new dog will love you. Besides," Christy
giggled, "it'll want you to keep it safe from
Lila!"

That made Ellie laugh so much that a
lady walking past with a big-eyed spaniel
gave her a funny look.

"Would you like a spaniel like that
one?" Christy asked. "They're quite small."

Ellie shook her head. "No, littler. What

I'd really like is a Jack Russell."

"Oh, they're really cute!"

Ellie thought for a moment. "Actually, I bet Mum would like a smaller dog. She always said we hadn't got the space when I asked before."

Christy grinned. "Then you'll just have to work on persuading the others!"

When Ellie got home, she looked through all her dog books and magazines to find out as much as she could about Jack Russells. She piled them up on the kitchen table, and waited.

When Dad got in from work, she offered to make him a cup of tea.

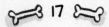

My Naughty Little Puppy

Mum laughed. "What are you after, Ellie?"

"I wanted to show you what sort of dog I'd like," she admitted. "A Jack Russell. Aren't they gorgeous? And they're small, too." She turned to the right page in her dog book.

Dad picked up the book. "I'd been thinking of a Westie, but I could see us with one of these..."

Mum frowned as she looked over Dad's shoulder. "It says they can be quite naughty."

"I think that's just because they get bored when they're left on their own," Ellie told her quickly. "I'd take ours for lots of walks. And even when I'm at school you're at home, Mum."

My Naughty Little Puppy

Max came in, looking very muddy.
"Is tea ready? I'm starving!
Hey, Dad. Are we
going to decide
on a dog?"
He peered
over at the book.
"A Jack Russell?"
He shook his
head. "We
want a big
dog! Little dogs can't go on proper walks."

"Jack Russells love walking!" Ellie
protested. "And they're clever, Max," she
added, searching for the magazine she
wanted. "You could teach our puppy
tricks, look."

My Naughty Little Puppy

Max looked at the picture Ellie had
found, which showed a really cheeky-
looking puppy leaping a metre in the air
to catch a Frisbee in its mouth. "Maybe.
Frisbee would be cool."

But Ellie had a feeling it was going
to be harder to persuade her sister.

When Lila came down for tea she
showed everyone a red setter photo she'd
printed off from a website.

Mum shook her head. "They're such big
dogs, Lila. And all that long fur, we'd have
to groom it every day."

"I'd do it!" Lila said.

"Every day?" Dad raised an eyebrow.

Lila nodded, but she was looking a
bit doubtful.

My Naughty Little Puppy

"Sorry, I just don't think we have the space," Mum said gently.

"Lila, look." Ellie had her secret weapon prepared. One of her dog magazines had a feature on clothes for dogs, with a photo of a super-cute Jack Russell posing in sunglasses and a little denim coat. Ellie thought it looked a bit silly, but she was sure Lila would like it.

"Aww!" Lila laughed.

My Naughty Little Puppy

"I don't think they make cute coats red-setter-sized," Ellie pointed out. "Only for little dogs."

Dad smiled and exchanged glances with Mum. "Right. Who's coming to help me find a Jack Russell breeder on the computer then?"

Chapter Three

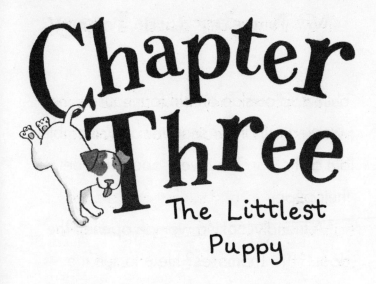

The Littlest Puppy

They had found a breeder on the internet who lived in a farmhouse just outside town. Dad had called them and arranged to go and see the litter of puppies the very next day. He seemed just as keen as Ellie to get a dog! Ellie peered out of the car window, over Lila's shoulder, to see if they were almost there yet. As the littlest she always had to sit in the middle seat.

They turned down a narrow track and

My Naughty Little Puppy

pulled up outside an old farmhouse. Ellie
wrestled out of her seat belt and scrambled
out of the car. They were about to meet
their puppy!

A friendly-looking woman opened the
door. "The Thomases? Here to see the
puppies? I'm Liz. Come on through. The
puppies have a little room just off the
kitchen."

Lila and Max chattered away to Liz, as
she led them into the house. Ellie tried to
follow them, but somehow everyone was
blocking the door to the puppy room.

"Max, can I see?" She tried to squeeze
round Max, but he wasn't listening.

Ellie sighed crossly. Sometimes she
hated being the smallest. Even Mum and

My Naughty Little Puppy

Dad were cooing over the puppies, and hadn't noticed she was still in the kitchen. She wasn't even going to get the chance to see the puppies before Lila and Max chose which one they were having!

She sat down on one of the kitchen chairs, and stared sadly at a dog magazine that was open on the table.

Suddenly, something damp pressed itself against her hand, and Ellie squeaked. Then the something nibbled her fingers hopefully. Ellie peered under the table.

There was a puppy down there!

He looked up at her hopefully with twinkly dark eyes, his floppy ears twitching as he put his head to one side.

 25

My Naughty Little Puppy

Ellie giggled. His expression was so naughty!

"Are you meant to be under there?" she whispered.

The puppy whined apologetically and licked her hand. His tongue was all soft and slobbery.

Just then, Ellie realized that the excited chatter from inside the puppy room had died down.

"Hang on. Can everyone just check for me... There should be five..." said Liz, sounding worried. "I don't believe it. He's got out again. I don't know how he climbs over the board in the doorway, none of the others can!"

Ellie looked down at the puppy.

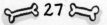

My Naughty Little Puppy

"She's talking about you, isn't she?" The puppy stared back at her with big, innocent eyes. *Who, me?* he seemed to be saying.

Ellie reached for the puppy, feeling a tiny bit worried that he wouldn't want to be picked up, but he seemed delighted to scramble into her arms. Cradling him against her shoulder, she stood up and walked over to the door.

"Um, is this who you're looking for?" Ellie went red. She wasn't very good at talking to strangers.

The puppy snuffled delightedly into her ear, making her squeak. Liz laughed and shook her head. "There he is! He's a real little rascal. He's obviously taken to you, though!"

"He's lovely!" Ellie said shyly.

My Naughty Little Puppy

Liz nodded. "Yes, he is. He's such a character. But he's just a bit too bouncy for some people. He's actually had one home already, with an older couple. I'm afraid they brought him back after two days. They took one of his sisters instead; she was a bit quieter."

My Naughty Little Puppy

The puppy's mum, Cleo, watched carefully as Ellie brought her baby back. She gave a sharp yap, as if she was telling him off. But then she licked the runaway puppy lovingly when Ellie placed him down next to her.

Ellie sat down on the floor of the puppy room. The puppies were all gorgeous, mostly white like her puppy, but with different splashes of black or brown. Hers was white all over, except for a couple of spots, and a brown mask over his ears and the top of his face. It gave him a mischievous look, like a burglar.

Ellie's puppy went pattering off across the floor, stalking a red plastic ball that the biggest puppy was nosing at.

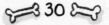

My Naughty Little Puppy

The biggest puppy, who was mostly
white with just one brown ear, nudged the
ball hard with his nose so that it went rolling
away. The two of them scampered after it,
but the rascally puppy
dashed ahead and
cornered the ball, his
tail wagging frantically
as he seized it in his
jaws. He whisked
round and came
trotting back to Ellie.
He then dropped the ball
into her lap, looking
remarkably pleased with himself.
It was half-deflated, with a neat little
set of teeth marks in its saggy side.

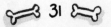

My Naughty Little Puppy

"He's brought you a present, Ellie!"
Dad commented.

"Dad, can we have this one? It's
definitely the nicest." Lila was holding up a
puppy with a black eyepatch like a pirate,
which was wriggling and squeaking as she
dangled it in the air.

My Naughty Little Puppy

Mum slipped a hand underneath the puppy. "Gently, sweetheart. They like a hand under their legs, or they feel nervous."

Max looked up. "Hey, no, can't we have this one?" He was playing tug-of-war with a rubber bone with the biggest puppy.

Ellie looked down at the naughty little puppy, who was now climbing into her lap after the ball. He heaved himself up her legs with a mighty effort and collapsed on top of the ball, his sides heaving. He gave an enormous yawn, then looked around him in confusion. Where was his ball now?

"I wish we could take you home," Ellie whispered to him. She knew that Lila and Max would argue if she tried to ask for this puppy instead, but a fiercely determined feeling was growing inside her. She usually didn't mind not getting her own way. She was used to it, and it was never about anything all that important. But this *was* important!

"I think *this* puppy's sweet," she started. "He's really clever. And I think he'd make us laugh."

"We don't want a dog to make us laugh!" Lila said rather scornfully.

"Why not?" Dad replied. "He is very cute. And he's really fallen for Ellie, look."

The puppy had worked out where the ball was now, and he was curled up on Ellie's knee, slumped over the ball, fast asleep.

My Naughty Little Puppy

"But Dad, I want this one!" Lila cradled
the pirate puppy, who was wriggling
grumpily.

"Ellie's puppy's cute, but it's the littlest,"
said Max. "We want a big, strong dog."

Ellie looked down at the puppy in
her lap. So what if he was little? He
would grow!

My Naughty Little Puppy

"They're all lovely." Mum smiled, and gently patted Ellie's puppy on the head. "But I agree, I think this puppy is the one for us."

Dad arranged with Liz that they would come back tomorrow to pick the puppy up.

"Can't we take him now?" Ellie asked hopefully.

"No, first we need to get him a basket, puppy food... Er ... all those kinds of things," Dad said uncertainly.

"I'll give you a list," Liz told them, smiling. "You'll be surprised how much stuff you need, even for one very small dog!"

Chapter Four

The Great
Name Question

Lila and Max squabbled in the car all the way home. They certainly weren't happy about their little sister getting to choose the new puppy.

"Will you two just stop it!" Dad snapped in the end. "How exactly did you think you were *both* going to get the puppy you wanted, even if we hadn't chosen Ellie's favourite? It's not as though we're getting two puppies! And this is a family dog, remember – for all of us!"

"We should have picked mine..." Lila grumbled.

"Mine was better!"

"That's enough!" Dad was using his I-really-mean-it voice, and Lila and Max fell silent.

Ellie tried not to smile too much. But she couldn't help it. They were getting a puppy tomorrow! Her favourite puppy, the one who had liked *her*! And if Max and Lila were going to sulk, maybe she would be able to do most of the looking after!

As soon as they got back, Ellie begged to nip over to see Grandad to tell him their exciting news. He lived round the corner from them, and he loved dogs too, even though he said he was too old to look after a dog these days. He had a cat instead, a big tabby called Freda.

"OK then," said Mum. "But not for long, Ellie. We need to go to the pet shop, remember."

"I'll be back soon," Ellie promised, as she opened the front door. "I just want to tell him our puppy's coming tomorrow. I still really want to come and help choose everything!"

She hurried down the road to Grandad's house and headed round to the side gate. In sunny weather like this, he was bound to be sitting out in the garden.

My Naughty Little Puppy

"Hi, Grandad!"

Grandad looked up from his deckchair, pleased to see her. "Hello, Ellie! You look excited. What's the big news?"

"We're getting a puppy! Tomorrow!"

My Naughty Little Puppy

"Your dad mentioned he was thinking about getting a dog. Well, that was fast work! So, what kind are you getting?"

"He's a Jack Russell."

Grandad nodded. "I had a Jack Russell, years ago. Smokey, he was called. They're real little characters. You're in for some fun."

"Lila wanted a red setter, but Mum and Dad wanted a small dog. And then at the breeders today, one of the puppies found me, Grandad, and he went to sleep in my lap. And he's the one we're having. The puppy I chose!" Ellie frowned suddenly. "Smokey's a really sweet name. I wonder what we're going to call our puppy?"

My Naughty Little Puppy

Grandad laughed as Ellie went dancing round the garden. Then she dashed over and gave him a hug. "I have to go now. We've got to buy all the stuff we need. Come and see us tomorrow, won't you? You have to meet our puppy!"

Ellie had hoped that it would be just her and Mum going to the pet shop, but Lila decided to come, too.

"This purple one's nice." Ellie pointed to a squashy dog bed with a paw-print pattern.

"You can't give a boy dog a purple bed!" Lila said. "The red one's good."

My Naughty Little Puppy

Ellie didn't see why red was any more
boyish than purple, but she knew better
than to bother arguing. She liked the red
bed anyway, and so did Mum.

They were just trying to work out which
colour of collar would suit the puppy best,
when Lila's mobile rang. "Mum, can I go
round to Rosie's?" she asked.

My Naughty Little Puppy

"As long as you're home for tea," said Mum.

"Don't you want to get things for the puppy?" Ellie asked, but Lila had quickly put a blue collar back on to the hook and was already practically out of the shop. Ellie looked hopefully at Mum. "Can we get the red one?"

Mum smiled. "I think he'd look perfect in red."

"We need a tag, too," said Ellie, looking down at Liz's list. She led Mum over to a little display of different collar-tags. "We could have a bone-shaped one!"

"That's lovely." Mum added the tag to her basket. "We'll have to get it engraved with his name and our phone number."

My Naughty Little Puppy

"But Mum, we still don't have a name!"
said Ellie.

When everyone was back home at
teatime, Mum asked if they had any ideas
of what to call their puppy.

"Ben," Max said immediately.

Ellie's nose wrinkled. Ben was OK, but it
didn't fit the puppy somehow.

"No, Lucky!" Lila protested.

"Lucky's a stupid name," Max growled.
"Besides, half the dogs in the park are
called Lucky. We want something different."

Mum nodded. "I agree. But I don't think
Ben's that different either. What about –
um – Sidney?"

My Naughty Little Puppy

"No!" Ellie squeaked in horror. He just wasn't a Sidney at all!

Dad laughed. "Well, what do you think then, Ellie?"

Ellie frowned. She wanted something just right. Something that fitted his naughty character and his burglar's mask. Suddenly, she remembered what Liz had said when

Ellie had found the puppy. "What about Rascal?" she suggested. "He has those markings across his face that make him look like a burglar."

My Naughty Little Puppy

Mum murmured it to herself a couple of times, and looked over at Dad. "I like it. What do you think?"

He nodded. "Nice and different."

Lila was frowning. "Lucky's better. But I suppose it's OK."

Max grinned. "Rascal... He looks naughty enough for it to fit."

Ellie nodded. "A real little rascal, that's what Liz called him!"

Chapter Five

Rascal Comes Home

Ellie carefully laid the fleecy paw-print blanket in the bottom of the pet carrier that they'd bought yesterday. She couldn't believe they were about to go and pick up their puppy!

"Can't we just hold him?" asked Lila, as Dad put the carrier in the boot.

Ellie had been thinking the same thing. It wasn't a very long drive.

But Dad shook his head. "What if he

My Naughty Little Puppy

got loose and started jumping around? From the look of that puppy, he'd be trying to climb out of the windows."

Ellie giggled. She could just imagine Rascal's waggy little bottom disappearing out of a car window, as he tried to see what was going on outside.

When they arrived at Liz's house, Dad brought the pet carrier in, and Liz took them straight to the puppy room. "Just be a little quiet," she warned them. "Your puppy has been in a pet carrier before, when I took him to the vet for his first set of vaccinations, and when he went to his first home, but it's still a bit worrying for him. We want to try and keep him calm." She stepped gently into the puppy room, and

My Naughty Little Puppy

Ellie and the others leaned round the door.
The puppies were asleep, all snuggled
up in a soft, wobbly pile. Cleo was curled
round them, and she pricked up her ears as
Liz went in.

My Naughty Little Puppy

"Hey, Cleo," Liz murmured, as she gently picked up the puppy. Ellie watched anxiously, wondering if Cleo understood what was happening. But she didn't seem to be upset. She just looked up sleepily.

"Doesn't she mind him going?" Ellie whispered, as Liz brought the drowsy puppy out of the room, and carefully slipped him into the pet carrier.

Liz shook her head. "No. Now that the puppies are twelve weeks old and they're having solid food, she's starting to think of them as grown-ups. Or teenagers, anyway! I think she's getting a bit sick of them climbing all over her, to be honest. She's probably looking forward to some peace and quiet when they've gone."

My Naughty Little Puppy

Rascal was awake now. He stared out
of the front of his carrier and gave a
worried little moan. Ellie crouched down in
front of him, whispering soothingly. The
moaning noises stopped, and he wagged
his tail. Or at least Ellie thought he did; it
was only the tiniest movement.

My Naughty Little Puppy

"Well done, Ellie," Dad said, lifting up the pet carrier to take it to the car. But even though Dad tried to carry it carefully, the puppy started moaning again as he felt the carrier swing.

Dad placed the carrier in the boot. As soon as he started the car, Rascal let out an enormous bark – it sounded far too loud for such a tiny dog. And then another, and another, all the way home.

Dad brought the pet carrier inside. "Thank goodness he's stopped barking!" he said, as he set it down on the kitchen floor.

Rascal was going to stay in the kitchen, as Liz had suggested keeping him in just

one room to start with. Although he was almost house-trained, he might have accidents in a new place. Mum definitely wanted him on a tiled floor! She placed some newspaper in the corner for Rascal to use if no one was there to let him out into the garden.

Lila swooped to open the carrier before Ellie or Max could get there. She reached inside, but Rascal backed away and whimpered.

"Don't scare him!" Ellie put in.

"I'm not!" Lila said crossly. "I'm only getting him out." She looked up at Ellie, a confused expression on her face, as though she didn't expect *Ellie* to be telling her what to do.

There was a questioning little whine that made them both look back down at the pet carrier. Rascal was standing at the door now, staring up at them uncertainly.

"Hey, Rascal," Ellie breathed. The puppy placed one cautious paw on to the floor. But he was looking up at her as he did it, and he tripped, rolling out of the carrier with a squeak. Ellie scooped him up and snuggled him close. "Silly boy," she murmured, and he licked her cheek.

"Look, do you want to see your new home?" Ellie put Rascal down, and he went pattering off across the kitchen to sniff the shoes that were by the back door.

"Uurgh, don't, Rascal! Dad's trainers might poison you!" Max tried to shoo him

My Naughty Little Puppy

away, but Rascal grabbed the trailing
laces, and set off across the floor, dragging
the shoe behind him. It was almost as big
as he was!

My Naughty Little Puppy

"Hey, Rascal, I need that!" Dad picked up the puppy, laughing. "I think we might have to move all those trainers. Looks like he might be a shoe-chewer." He put Rascal down on the other side of the kitchen.

Next, the puppy inspected his new bowls. There wasn't anything in his food bowl, and he looked up mournfully.

"Soon," Dad promised. "Where's that timetable Liz gave us?"

"I've stuck it up on the fridge." Mum went over to take a look. "Yes, he's supposed to have a small bowl of those special biscuits now."

When he saw the bag, Rascal gave a squeaky little yap and scampered round his food bowl, his whole back end wagging.

My Naughty Little Puppy

Max laughed. "He must be starving!"

"Urgh, that food smells disgusting," Lila complained, fanning a hand in front of her nose.

Ellie smiled to herself. It didn't smell wonderful, but it wasn't that bad. At least it looked like Lila wouldn't be fighting to feed Rascal.

Rascal was so excited when Mum poured out the biscuits that he practically dived into the bowl, tipping it over. A wave of dog biscuits poured out. The puppy sat down in the middle of them with a bump, looking confused. What had happened to his lunch?

Everyone laughed, and he looked up, whining.

My Naughty Little Puppy

"He thinks we're cross..." Ellie crouched down and tried to scoop some of the food back into his bowl. "It's OK, you eat it up," she said gently.

But Rascal preferred to eat off the floor. He snuffled round the edge of his bowl like a little Hoover, gobbling up any stray biscuits. Then he carefully put his front paws right inside the bowl to finish off the rest, in case it tried to get away again.

"He's going to get himself covered when he has those special tins and this milky stuff," Max pointed out, reading the timetable.

My Naughty Little Puppy

"I bet the tins smell even worse." Lila
made a face.

"I'll wash him if he gets messy," Ellie
said eagerly. "I don't mind."

She was kneeling down still, and
suddenly determined little paws were
clambering up her leg. Ellie put a hand
under Rascal's bottom to help him. His
tummy looked like a little balloon; Ellie was
almost sure she could see the outlines of
the dog biscuits against his white fur. He
slumped gratefully on to her lap and
sighed, his eyes closing almost immediately.

Lila looked at him warily and
shuddered. "Be careful, Ellie. He ate that
ever so fast. Just watch out he doesn't throw
up all over you!"

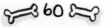

Chapter Six

A Noisy Night

Ellie lay in bed, hugging her old bear. It had been a wonderful first day with Rascal. Ellie, Max and Lila had spent ages playing with him, and Grandad had come round to admire the new arrival, too. Ellie was exhausted from all the fun they'd had. But she couldn't sleep. Not with those sad noises coming from downstairs.

Poor little Rascal! Mum had said he would be fine; they just had to leave him to

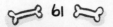

My Naughty Little Puppy

get used to his new home. But it was so
unfair that he had to be shut up all alone in
the kitchen. He was used to having his mum,
and his brothers and sisters to snuggle up
next to. Of course he was upset!

Ellie crept out on to the landing and
hung over the banister rail. The howling
noises weren't stopping, and Rascal had
started scratching at the kitchen door.

My Naughty Little Puppy

"Mum, I'm trying to watch TV, and I can't hear a thing!" Max moaned from the living room.

Dad snorted. "Now you know how I feel when you've got your mates round!"

"It's time you were going to bed, anyway, Max," said Mum.

"Between him howling and Lila turning her music up so she can't hear him, how am I supposed to sleep?" Max grumbled.

The living room door was flung open, and Ellie just managed to make it back to her room before Max stomped up the stairs.

She picked up her bear and climbed back into bed. That was what Rascal needed, something to cuddle! Ellie looked down at the bear, thoughtfully. It was one of those hottie bears, with a middle bit full of special lavender-scented beans you could heat up in the microwave. If she warmed it and gave it to Rascal, wouldn't that feel just like another dog?

Mum opened the bedroom door to check on her, and Ellie quickly flopped down and pretended to be asleep.

But after Mum and Dad had been in bed for a while, Ellie sneaked over to her door and opened it carefully. There was no noise from any of the bedrooms, just the occasional miserable howl from downstairs. She crept along the landing, feeling a bit guilty. She was supposed to be fast asleep by now, but making Rascal feel better was more important.

My Naughty Little Puppy

She tiptoed down the stairs and let
herself into the kitchen. Rascal was just a
white shape in the darkness, and he
whimpered uncertainly.

"It's OK," Ellie whispered. "I've got
something to cheer you up."

My Naughty Little Puppy

Rascal climbed out of his bed, and pattered over to her, as she put the bag of scented beans into the microwave. "I'm making you a dog to cuddle. Just like your mum," she explained. She crouched down and picked Rascal up, and he sighed gratefully. He watched the bag revolving in the microwave with interest, as though it might be food.

"There you go..." Ellie slipped the bag inside the bear. Then she crouched down and carefully arranged it in his bed so he could snuggle up next to it.

But when she put Rascal back into his bed, he climbed straight out again, and into her lap. Ellie giggled. "No, no, you're supposed to cuddle up with the bear."

My Naughty Little Puppy

Rascal obviously didn't think the bear was very much like his mum.

"I suppose your mum isn't lavender-scented," Ellie said, watching as he curled up to sleep — on her lap.

"Rascal, my foot's going to sleep!" she whispered. But Rascal looked so worn out, she couldn't bear to move.

My Naughty Little Puppy

Ellie woke up with a start as her mum switched on the kitchen light.

"Ellie, what are you doing in here? It's half-past one in the morning!" she whispered.

"Ow..." Ellie murmured. She'd fallen asleep leaning against the cupboard with her legs crossed, and now they ached. So did her bottom.

Mum carefully put the fast-asleep puppy into his basket. "I just went to the loo and I noticed that your door was open. When I saw that you weren't in bed I had a good idea where you'd got to... I told you we had to leave Rascal to get used to the kitchen!"

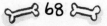

My Naughty Little Puppy

Ellie nodded sleepily. "I'm sorry.
I wanted to give Rascal my hottie bear —
to be like his mum, you see? But he didn't
like it..." She gave a massive yawn.

Mum sighed and helped Ellie to her
feet. "Come on, you need to go back to
sleep!"

She was less cross by the morning, but
Mum made Ellie promise that she wouldn't
do it again. "Besides, he was perfectly
happy when I came down this morning,"
Mum pointed out.

"What happened to my bear?" Ellie
asked, looking down at Rascal's empty
bed. "Oh no!" She crawled under the
table, and pulled out a decidedly worse-
for-wear bear.

My Naughty Little Puppy

"Oh dear. He's chewed that ribbon to bits. I'm going to have to cut it off." Mum shook her head. "And his ear will need stitching back."

Rascal looked up at Ellie with big dark eyes, and Ellie sighed. "You definitely are a Rascal, aren't you? What was wrong with my nice bear?"

"We'll have to be careful about leaving things lying around," Mum said. "Especially once he's allowed out of the kitchen. You lot are all going to have to put your school bags away, or the dog really will eat your homework!"

Chapter Seven
Disaster at the Vet's

Ellie spent most of the morning on the kitchen floor, playing with Rascal. Max and Lila both joined in for a bit, but then Lila went off to the cinema with some friends, and a mate of Max's came round to go skateboarding.

Ellie shook her head. "I don't know why they want to go out," she told Mum. "They're missing all this time with Rascal!"

Just then, Christy rang the doorbell.

My Naughty Little Puppy

Ellie was desperate to show Rascal off,
and Mum had agreed that Christy could
come round straight after her morning
walk with Bouncer.

"I need to go and do some work," said
Mum. "You girls will be all right on your
own, won't you?"

Rascal peered curiously round the leg
of the kitchen table, as Christy came into
the room. "Oh, Ellie, he's gorgeous!" she
said.

"Just make sure you keep your new
trainers away from him!" Ellie warned.

Rascal trotted over to Christy. She held
out her hand for him to smell and he gave it
a gentle lick.

"He likes you," said Ellie, as Christy

My Naughty Little Puppy

bowled a ball of rolled-up newspaper
towards the puppy. Rascal leaped on it,
growling fiercely and tearing it with his little
white teeth. "I hope he gets
on with Bouncer, too."

My Naughty Little Puppy

"He's so tiny, Bouncer's going to have to be careful not to squash him." Christy giggled. "Oh, look, we'd better clear up all that paper before your mum comes back."

After playing all afternoon, Rascal had keeled over in the middle of a game and fallen asleep, half on Ellie and half on Christy.

"He's like a toy dog when he's sleeping," Christy whispered, as she gently edged him further on to Ellie. "Bye, Rascal! Why don't you ask your mum if you can take him for a walk tomorrow morning with me and Bouncer?"

Ellie sighed. "I wish we could, but Rascal's got to have his last lot of vaccinations before he's allowed out. We're taking him to the vet's tomorrow, though."

She waved Christy off from her place on the floor, then stroked Rascal's head, just with one finger. His fur was so smooth and soft.

Christy had only just left, when Ellie heard Lila come home.

"Hey, Rascal," said Lila, opening the kitchen door.

Straight away, Rascal opened his eyes. He stood up on Ellie's lap, barking excitedly.

Ellie frowned. Her leg felt funny. Sort of warm ... and wet...

"Uuurgh, Rascal!" Ellie groaned. "You're supposed to use the newspaper for that, remember!"

My Naughty Little Puppy

Lila stared at her in horror. "Did he wee on you?"

Ellie lifted Rascal off her damp jeans and nodded. She carried Rascal over to his newspapers. "Here, look, on the newspaper..." Rascal looked round at her apologetically and gave his tail a tiny wag. "It's OK, I'm not cross. I'm going to have to go and change, though!"

Lila shook her head and giggled. "I can't believe he weed on you! Rather you than me, Ellie!"

Ellie lifted Rascal out of his pet carrier and clipped on his lead, just in case he wriggled out of her arms in the vet's. Rascal was looking around eagerly, his tail wagging with excitement.

Ellie laughed. "It's only the vet's car park, Rascal! I just can't wait to take him for a proper walk, Mum."

"It won't be long now. We need to wait a week for the vaccinations to work, that's all."

"Oh, I thought he'd be able to go out straight away. A week is ages," Ellie said sadly. "It'll be almost the end of the holidays by then. And Christy's going to be really disappointed, too."

"You'll still be able to walk him after school once you go back," said Mum. "And Christy can come over to play with him whenever she wants."

The vet's waiting room was empty, apart from one lady with a cat basket, sitting in the corner. Ellie and Mum sat down to wait for their turn, and Rascal sniffed around their chairs, fascinated by all the strange smells.

It wasn't long before he noticed the cat basket, and he eyed it eagerly. Before Ellie could stop him, he'd pulled the lead from her hands and scampered over to

take a look. Ellie dashed after him and
grabbed the lead, just as Rascal poked his
nose through the bars.

"Rascal, I wouldn't—"

There was a burst of angry hissing. Then
a sharp-clawed paw shot out of the front of
the basket, sending Rascal reeling
backwards, right into a display stand of
leaflets, which scattered all over the floor.

My Naughty Little Puppy

The cat's owner glared at Ellie, and
Rascal scuttled back to her, whimpering.
Mum quickly started to pick up the leaflets,
looking embarrassed.

Ellie cuddled Rascal tightly and
whispered in his ear. "Shh, it's all right." She
lowered her voice even more. "It's a
horrible mean cat, just leave it alone."

"I should have known he'd be trouble,"
Mum sighed, as she replaced the last of
the leaflets. "I only hope it's our turn soon."

Chapter Eight

The Ham Thief

Mum had arranged ages ago for Auntie Gemma to take Ellie and Lila shopping that Friday. (Max had been invited too, but he'd said he'd rather have his fingers cut off.) Ellie was a bit worried about leaving Rascal, even though he'd been fine since his injections. She'd been out without him, of course, but only for short walks with Christy and Bouncer, and to the shops with Mum. This was a whole day. Still, he'd have Mum and Max.

My Naughty Little Puppy

Auntie Gemma made a big fuss of
Rascal. But she wasn't too happy when she
realized he'd chewed through the leather
thong holding the charm on to her handbag,
which she'd unwisely left under the table.
"Don't worry, I suppose it won't be too hard
to mend," Auntie Gemma said, as Ellie
apologized. "Shall we get going, girls?"

My Naughty Little Puppy

Ellie missed Rascal, even though they had a lovely time shopping. Auntie Gemma bought her a gorgeous purple T-shirt, and a red one for Lila. Then Ellie persuaded her to take them to a pet shop, where she got Rascal a special chew toy with a space to put dog treats in. Ellie wanted to make up for leaving him behind.

For lunch, Auntie Gemma took the girls to a pizza restaurant. Normally, pizza was Ellie's favourite, but she just couldn't help thinking about what Rascal was doing without her. She picked at her food, wondering if Rascal would like pepperoni. It felt strange not to have him begging by

My Naughty Little Puppy

her chair for Ellie to feed him little titbits when Mum wasn't looking. She hoped Mum had remembered to give him all his special meals, and to wash off the sticky porridge one from his ears before it set.

Ellie raced up the path when they got home, and rang repeatedly on the doorbell.

"I'm coming, I'm coming," came Mum's voice. She opened the front door, looking harassed.

"Oh, I'm glad you're back, Ellie!"

"What is it? Is Rascal OK?"

"Well, he sat by the kitchen door and moaned the whole day – when he wasn't howling! Max tried to cheer him up, but I think he just wanted you. Oh, I've got such a headache."

My Naughty Little Puppy

There was a whimpering and
scrabbling sound coming from the kitchen,
and Rascal threw himself at Ellie as soon
as she opened the door.

"Just look at those scratches on the
paintwork!" Mum cried.

Auntie Gemma laughed. "I think you
named him just right, Ellie!"

"Rascal, no! Ellie, catch him, please!" Mum
sounded cross. Rascal was sick of being
shut in the kitchen, and was getting clever
at sneaking out whenever anyone opened
the door even a crack. "If he escapes
again, then no walk today!"

Ellie carefully shooed Rascal back in.

My Naughty Little Puppy

"Sorry, Rascal! This is your room." She turned to her mum. "You didn't mean what you said about not going for a walk?" she asked worriedly.

Mum sighed. "No, I suppose not. And we probably should start letting him out of the kitchen now he's settled in. But he got halfway up the stairs twice last night, before your dad caught him. I think he wants to be with you."

Ellie imagined Rascal asleep on her bed. She looked at her mum hopefully. "Could I ... just once?"

"No! And don't think I won't notice if you try and sneak him into your room. He sheds those white hairs everywhere he goes!"

Rascal looked over at Mum with big brown eyes, as she opened the fridge door. "Oh, yes, you're very cute, but you're not getting round me. Don't try and pretend you're starving, just because I've got the fridge open." She frowned. "There should be some ham in here I was going to use for lunch. Max must've eaten it!"

Ellie opened her mouth and then shut it again, as Max came into the kitchen.

"Mum! I'm starving, what's for lunch?"

Mum glared at Max. "How can you possibly be hungry when you've eaten all that ham that was in here? Toast is what you'll be getting now; there's nothing left for sandwiches!"

"I didn't eat it!" Max protested.

Mum folded her arms. "Like you didn't eat that whole packet of biscuits last week?"

"I did take the biscuits, I told you I did, but not the ham. This is so unfair!"

"Fine. No lunch," Mum snapped.

"Um, Mum..." Ellie muttered. "It was me..."

My Naughty Little Puppy

Mum looked at her wide-eyed. "You ate half a packet of ham? Ellie, you don't even like ham. I always have to do Marmite for you!"

"Rascal likes it," Ellie whispered.

Mum looked down at Rascal, sitting innocently by Ellie's feet. "You fed it to Rascal? All of it?"

"He was hungry..." Ellie stared down at the floor. She wasn't used to Mum being cross with her. "And I thought he might need a little extra, with his first proper walk this afternoon. Sorry, Mum."

My Naughty Little Puppy

"Ellie, you'll make him sick if you overfeed him," Mum explained. "You really mustn't give him anything that isn't his proper food. And don't take food out of the fridge without asking!" She frowned. "You'd better both be angels from now on, or the walk really can wait for another day!"

Ellie nodded. "I will, and Rascal will too, I promise!"

"I just hope he isn't sick," Mum muttered.

"Hey, what about me?" Max put in. "What am I going to have to eat if Rascal's had all the ham?"

Chapter Nine

Rascal's First Walk

"Can we go yet?" Ellie asked hopefully. Mum seemed to have been pottering about for ages. Luckily, the ham didn't seem to have upset Rascal's stomach, and Ellie had managed to hide her pair of flip-flops that Rascal had stolen from under her chair during lunch. Hopefully she could stick the flowery bits back on before Mum noticed.

"Why don't you get his lead, Ellie, while I finish my cup of tea?" Mum smiled at her.

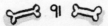

My Naughty Little Puppy

Just then, Max came in dangling Rascal's red lead, and Ellie's face fell. Of course Max and Lila would want to walk Rascal too. She'd forgotten that, imagining it would be just her and Mum.

Rascal looked at the lead uncertainly, and Ellie wondered if he remembered his trip to the vet's. But he let Max clip it on. "Come on, Rascal," Max called, leading him to the front door. Mum and Ellie followed, and Lila ran down the stairs to join them.

However, when Max opened the front door, Rascal let out a frightened little squeak. He sat down on his bottom and wriggled backwards when Max tried to yank at the lead.

My Naughty Little Puppy

"Rascal, walk! Come on, we're going to
the park!" Max said.

My Naughty Little Puppy

Ellie stifled a giggle, and Max glared at her. "You do it then, if it's so funny!" He handed her the lead.

She crouched down next to Rascal, and stroked him gently. "Shall we go for a walk, Rascal?" she murmured. Then Ellie dropped one of his special dog biscuits just below the doorstep. "Come on, sweetheart."

Rascal stepped down to snatch the biscuit, and crunched it up. Then he sniffed at the plants by the side of the path, and took a cautious step forward.

"She cheated," Max muttered.

Ellie practised walking Rascal round the front garden first, and then they set off down the road. But it was a very slow walk, because Rascal wasn't really used to his lead. In the end, Ellie carried him most of the way to the park, which luckily wasn't far away.

When they reached the gate, Rascal stopped and stared at the huge space, dotted with trees, with a hill leading down to the big pond at the bottom. Lots of other dogs were running around, and it looked like dog heaven.

Rascal pulled excitedly on the lead and barked loudly as a huge black Labrador came snuffling past. Ellie laughed. "Let's run!" They dashed off across the grass, Max, Lila and Mum racing after them. Everyone laughed at Rascal as he bounced along, jumping so he could see over the long grass.

My Naughty Little Puppy

Finally, Rascal stopped and sat panting at Ellie's feet.

"Aww, he's worn out!" Lila laughed.

But suddenly, Rascal's ears pricked up. He was staring down the hill at the ducks waddling and flapping around the reeds at the edge of the pond. He shook himself briskly and set off down the slope, his tail wagging madly with excitement. Ellie raced after him, skidding and sliding as they sped through the grass.

"Ellie, no!" Mum shouted.

Ellie tried to stop, pulling hard on the lead, but Rascal was too interested in the ducks. They'd noticed him now, and were starting to quack anxiously, fluttering their feathers and slip-sliding into the water as

My Naughty Little Puppy

fast as they could.

"Not in the water! Rascal, stop!" Ellie
gasped.

And he did, skidding to a halt just at the
edge, and barking crossly at the ducks as
they paddled away.

Unfortunately, Ellie was running so fast
that she stumbled. She wobbled on the
edge of the pond, before tumbling

My Naughty Little Puppy

forwards and sitting down with a splash, up to her chest in dirty, slimy pond water.

"Uurrgh!" Ellie groaned. "Don't look at me like that, Rascal, this is your fault. Oh, yuck, I'm sitting in duck poo!"

Max slid down the slope and stood laughing at her. "You're soaked!" He knelt down and stretched out a hand to help her up.

My Naughty Little Puppy

Rascal yapped sharply.

"Max, look out!" Ellie cried, as Rascal ran up to Max and scrabbled at the back of his legs, knocking him off balance.

Mum and Lila arrived just as Max toppled into the pond too, sending another wave of muddy water all over Ellie.

My Naughty Little Puppy

Lila sniggered, then backed off a few steps as Max and Ellie staggered out. "Don't you dare come anywhere near me!"

"What are you two *doing?*" Mum asked, staring at them in horror.

"I was trying to help!" Max protested. "I was pulling Ellie out, but Rascal jumped up at me."

"Oh dear." Mum shook her head. "Maybe he thought you were trying to hurt Ellie. He does seem to think she's his special person."

Even though she was soaking wet and covered in mud (and worse) Ellie felt like she was glowing inside.

She was Rascal's special person!

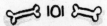

Chapter Ten

A Night Visitor

"I just don't know what to do with him, Grandad!" Ellie sighed, watching as Rascal investigated Grandad's garden. She'd brought him round for some advice. Grandad had kept Freda shut inside. Ellie wasn't sure Rascal was ready to meet another cat just yet!

"What's he been up to?" Grandad asked her.

"We took him for his first walk yesterday,

to the park." Ellie went red. "He was really naughty." She told Grandad about the pond incident, which made him laugh.

"Isn't it normally the dog that gets all wet and muddy on a walk, not its owner?" he joked.

"I'm taking him out again later, with Christy. I just hope he's a bit better behaved. Everyone's getting a little grumpy with him," Ellie said finally. "He ate one of Dad's slippers when we got home from the walk."

"Didn't you tell him off?" Grandad asked.

Ellie nodded. "Well, Dad did. I'm not very good at telling him off."

"But Rascal doesn't think he's your dad's dog, Ellie."

My Naughty Little Puppy

"Oh ... I see what you mean."

Grandad smiled. "If you're going to have all the love and the cuddles, then you need to do the hard stuff, too. And I don't just mean the falling in ponds, Ellie love. You need to be the one who makes Rascal behave."

Ellie watched Rascal trying to creep up on a butterfly. He was so gorgeous, but if he kept on being naughty, he'd be a terror when he was a grown-up dog. It was a *big* responsibility.

"This is going to be so cool!" Christy beamed, as Ellie opened the front door. She went to untie Bouncer's lead from the gate.

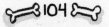

My Naughty Little Puppy

Ellie nodded. "I know. But we're not going anywhere near the pond, OK? I still smell of mud and I've had two baths since yesterday. Come on, Rascal!"

He pattered out of the front gate, looking very smart in his red collar and lead. Dad had got the little bone-shaped tag engraved with Rascal's name and their phone number.

"He's so tiny and Bouncer's so huge!" Ellie laughed as Rascal sniffed interestedly at Bouncer. "Oh, Rascal, don't sniff his bottom, that's rude!"

My Naughty Little Puppy

Bouncer sniffed Rascal back, and then gave him a friendly lick. His tongue covered Rascal's whole head, and Rascal gave a confused sneeze. He let out a sharp, cross bark, and Bouncer stepped back, his tail between his legs.

Christy burst out laughing. "Bouncer, you can't be scared of Rascal — you're ten times bigger than he is!"

Bouncer lay down with his nose on the pavement, his tail wagging. Rascal gave the bigger dog's nose an approving lick, and then they set off together down the road.

Ellie and Christy smiled at each other. It looked like Bouncer and Rascal had sorted things out for themselves.

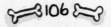

Ellie ended up carrying Rascal most of
the way to the park again, as he kept
getting tangled up in his lead.

"Has he done anything else awful
lately?" Christy asked, as they approached
the park gates.

"No! Well, he chewed my sketchbook this
morning. But only the edges..." she admitted.

My Naughty Little Puppy

"I tried to tell him off, like Grandad said. It's really hard. He looked so upset!"

"He'll turn into a monster if you never tell him off." Christy shook her head.

"I know. I really tried. Stern voice and everything, honestly." Ellie sighed. "But he just gives me this really sad look... I've just got to try harder, I suppose."

That night, Ellie lay in bed smiling sleepily to herself. She had loved walking with Christy and Bouncer and Rascal. It was so much more fun now that she had her own dog. Even though he had barked at every dog they walked past, and tried to climb a tree, chasing after a squirrel that was

My Naughty Little Puppy

almost bigger than he was!

There was a gentle scratching at her bedroom door, and suddenly it swung open. Ellie sat up, her half-asleep brain thinking of ghosts, and her heart thudding.

But the little white shape was no ghost. It was a puppy.

My Naughty Little Puppy

"Rascal! How did you open the kitchen door?" Ellie whispered. "Did Dad not shut it properly?"

Rascal put his paws on the side of her bed and looked at her hopefully. Ellie lifted him up. "We'll get in trouble if Mum finds out, so shhh!"

Rascal scrambled happily down the bed and curled up on Ellie's feet. He felt just like a heavy hot-water bottle.

Ellie sighed happily and snuggled down under her duvet. Her own little dog, sleeping on her bed. It was what she'd dreamed of.

"Sometimes I'm really glad you're naughty..." she whispered, and she drifted off to sleep, reminding herself to brush all the dog-hairs off her duvet in the morning...

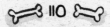

WOOF
Magazine

Out now

My Naughty Little Puppy

New Tricks for Rascal

Rascal's naughtiness is annoying everyone, so Mum and Dad decide it's time to take him to dog-training classes. Ellie thinks this is a brilliant plan. But wherever Rascal goes, trouble is never far behind...

Jack Russells: Small dog, BIG personality!

 Although this perky little pooch was originally bred as a hunting dog, he makes a great pet too. These dogs are brave, loyal and most of all they like to be the centre of attention!

 But they can be trained to perform tricks, and you'll find that your pet can jump higher than dogs twice his size! They are also very amusing and fun to be with, so you'll never have a dull day with one around.

 A lot of Jack Russell owners have fun dressing their pup up in funky jackets and T-shirts made to fit small dogs. But don't tell them that: Jack Russells think they are just as big as all the other dogs in the park!